A Perfect Day!

Story by Andrew S. Taylor
Illustrations by James G. Martin

Copyright © 2024 by Andrew S. Taylor
A Perfect Day!
Illustrated by James G. Martin

All rights reserved. No part of this work may be used or reproduced, transmitted, stored or used in any form or by any means graphic, electronic, or mechanical, including but not limited to photocopying, recording, scanning, digitizing, taping, Web distribution, information networks or information storage and retrieval systems, or in any manner whatsoever without prior written permission from the publisher.

An Imprint for GracePoint Publishing
(www.GracePointPublishing.com)

GracePoint Matrix, LLC
624 S. Cascade Ave, Suite 201
Colorado Springs, CO 80903
www.GracePointMatrix.com Email: Admin@GracePointMatrix.com
SAN # 991-6032

A Library of Congress Control Number has been requested and is pending.
ISBN: 978-1-961347-71-7
ISBN: 978-1-961347-72-4

Books may be purchased for educational, business, or sales promotional use.
For bulk order requests and price schedule contact:
Orders@GracePointPublishing.com

The sun is just peeking out over the mountains.

The son is just peeking out over the pillow.
The father, my Dad, has been up for over an hour.

He's got all the gear in the rear of the car and everything is in its proper place.

It's a perfect day waiting to happen.

We say, "Ready Rooney! It's breakfast time!"
Martin's Café: Take a greasy spoon, dip it in fat, and that's where it's at.
At the far end of "coronary row", the front counter, there are two empty seats.

My Dad and I saunter and sit next to the town's daily diners.
These mammoth, modern-day mountain men are all farmers by trade and tradition. They know and, "Hello!" every waitress.

They read, and talk about, every local newspaper.
All subjects get equal airtime: *Daily News*, *Sports*, *Arts & Entertainment*, and most important, *The Weather*.

As we listen to these network-news-show-rivals, my Dad drinks high-test-leaded-black coffee, eats 100% bran cereal, and reads *The Montana Daily*

The men get served the usual, right away, everyday. Their magnificent, mega-meal menus are right off the Weight-Watcher's-Breakfast-Don't-Dos-Taboos List!

I sweetly sugar-high myself with The Breakfast of Champions.
I drink a large glass of milk, a small glass of O.J., and the waitress describes my individual, incredibly-edible item as "a huge, hot, butter and icing, cin-full roll."

Then I spend the entire meal reading, listening, and laughing at *The Funnies*. These are the newspaper's comic column of cartoons, and my Dad's comic, color commentary.

It's a perfect day, happily happening.

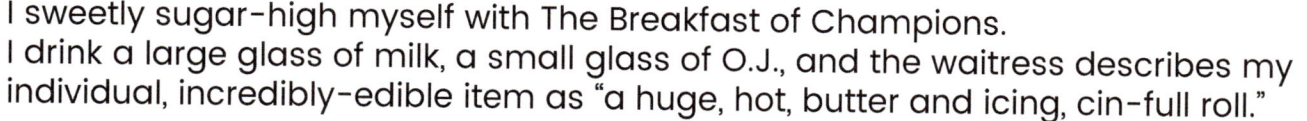

We say, "Ready Rooney! It's fishing time!"
We arrive at Armstrong's Farm, and yes, a river runs through it.

My Dad points out all the rolling riffles, connecting currents,

and placid pools.

Then, just like my Dad taught me, I set up my rod and reel, feel my way as I wade, pick a prime spot, and begin my methodical method of working the water.

All day, my Dad's never too far away.
He wants to stay near me.
He wants to hear my continued conversation.
He wants to help untangle any, "Great-Gordian-Knots!"

He wants to, "That's it!" and, "Well done!" any fantastic fish.
He wants to catch any fabulous photo-ops.
It's all day fun, being with my Dad.
And oh yea, the fishing is also fun.

And to beautifully bookend the best breakfast with the most delicious dinner, we each devour a super steak at The Livingston Bar & Grill.

Tomorrow's repeat performance is positvely planned.
And then it's back to the motel room for some much needed,
and definitely deserved relaxation, rest, and rejuvination.
After all, once again, tomorrow will be an early start.

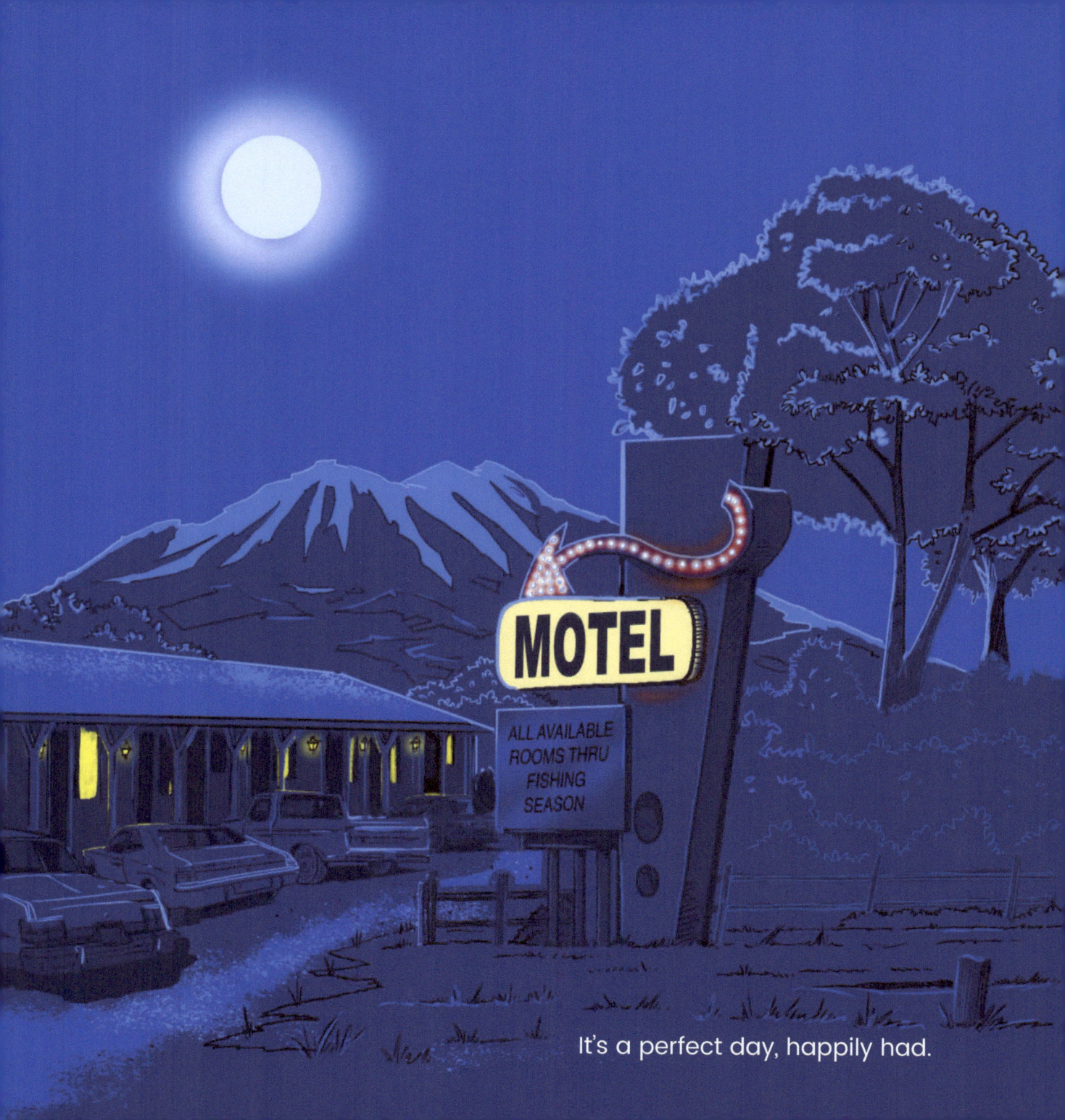
It's a perfect day, happily had.

Thanks for all these magical memories, Dad!

With an abundance of appreciation for:

Everyone at Mike Schultz Outfitters & Fly Shop and All Their Families,
AND... James Hughes & His Family!

THANKS FOR ALL THE FANTASTIC FISHING!

TaylorEDTime.com A+

About the Author

Andrew S. Taylor holds two BSED degrees in Pre-K-12, Elementary and Secondary Education Theater/Speech. As a self-employed entrepreneur, he is a teenage through adult Life Enrichment Teacher, Creativity Workshop Facilitator, Special Event Public Speaker, and Personal/Professional Life Coach/Consultant. He is equally proficient with individuals, couples, and large-scale groups. At Interlochen National Arts Camp, he was Divisional Honor Camper ('87 H.S.B. Theater Major) and Honor Cabin Counselor ('05 & '07). He was his university's Muppet Mascot, The OU Bobcat, a Pre-K-12 Child Care Teacher/Program Director for eight years, and also The Children's Department Supervisor & Storytime Reader, at a super-sized Barnes & Noble, for four years.

When not every day, enthusiastically engaged in creative writing, his hobbies include collating his colossal collection of Movies & TV Shows (2,800+DISKS!), making beaded jewelry (pins, necklaces, and friendship bracelets), and acting in Community Theater. Mr. Taylor lives in Ann Arbor, MI, and can be contacted at www.TaylorEDTime.com.

About the Illustrator

James G. Martin is a professional artist and illustrator with over thirty years of experience in product design for McDonald's Happy Meal toys, retail toys and holiday giftware. He has enjoyed working on the world's most popular licenses from Walt Disney Pictures, Pixar, DreamWorks, and Cartoon Network to name a few!

He resides in Kansas City, MO. with his family and their two dogs, Walter and Grubby. You can see more of his art at www.mrmartinart.com.

OTHER BOOKS BY ANDREW S. TAYLOR

BIRDS!

The Phenomenal Phoenix!

Something Small

A Cloud & The Eye of the Beholder

Mommy, Am I BEAUTIFUL?

LULLABY-ed Child

Sitting in the Lap of Love!

Every Day is Mother's Day: Sitting in the Sunroom of My Sweetest Sanctuary

Another Perfect Day! Every Day is Dad's Day

TaylorED Time: How to Dramatically Build Your Character
& Live the Life FANTASTIC!

TaylorED Time Workbook: How to Be the Captain
of Your Character's Creation

www.ingramcontent.com/pod-product-compliance
Lightning Source LLC
Chambersburg PA
CBHW041722040426
42451CB00003B/26